WIGGLESBOTTOM PRIMARY SUPER DOG

THERE'S LOADS MORE MAYHEM IN

WIGGLESBOTTOM PRIMARY

THE TOILET GHOST

THE SHARK IN THE POOL

THE MAGIC HAMSTER

WIGGLESBOTTOM PRIMARY
SUPER DOG

PAMELA BUTCHART
BECKA MOOR

nosy crow

WELCOME TO WIGGLESBOTTOM PRIMARY!

SUSIE
MR HARRIS
ROZ
SUNITA
GAVIN
ANNE-MARIE
JOEL
BOBBY
THEO

First published in 2017 by Nosy Crow Ltd
The Crow's Nest, 14 Baden Place,
Crosby Row, London SE1 1YW

www.nosycrow.com

ISBN: 978 0 85763 675 1

Nosy Crow and associated logos are trademarks and/or registered
trademarks of Nosy Crow Ltd

A CIP catalogue record for this book is available from the British Library.

Printed in Spain.

Papers used by Nosy Crow are made
from wood grown in
sustainable forests.

5 7 9 8 6

CONTENTS

FOR DOM, IAN,
LEN & THE CHICKENS!
THANK YOU FOR
EVERYTHING, DOM.
IT'S BEEN A HOOT!
P. B.

TO MANDY
AND JAY
B. M.

SUPER DOG

One time, a **DOG** got into the playground at morning break.

At first, we all thought it was a **WOLF** because it was **HUGE**. But Megan McNally said that it was **DEFINITELY NOT** a wolf because wolves are **WILD** so they don't wear collars.

The dog ran around the playground for ages and everyone **SCREAMED** whenever it came near them. But then Mr Harris, the deputy head, came out to see what all the **SCREAMING** was about and the dog disappeared.

EVERYONE was talking about the Playground Dog when we went back to the classroom and **NO ONE** could concentrate on their French like Miss Riley wanted us to do because we were all thinking about the dog.

Then Bobby Henderson gasped and pointed out of the window and shouted,

"HE'S BACK!"

But by the time we all got out of our seats and ran up to the window to see, Playground Dog had **DISAPPEARED** again.

Irfan Baxter said that it was a bit **WEIRD** how **BOTH TIMES** the dog had disappeared so quickly and that maybe Playground Dog had

That's when we all realised that this was

NO ORDINARY DOG.

At lunchtime, loads of people spotted Playground Dog in weird places and Megan McNally even thought she spotted his tail on the **ROOF**!

That's when Irfan said, "I can't believe it. **THAT'S** how he keeps disappearing. Playground Dog can **FLY!**"

Then Susie Keys shouted, "He's a **SUPER DOG!**"

And everyone gasped and someone started clapping. And then **EVERYONE** started clapping and shouting, **"SU-PER DOG! SU-PER DOG!"**

EVERYONE wanted to meet Super Dog but we didn't know what to do to stop him from flying away from us.

So that's when Susie Keys said that she would **SACRIFICE** her lunch so we could all meet Super Dog.

I didn't really know what that meant until Susie Keys took her cheese sandwich out of

her lunch box and shouted,

Nothing happened for a bit. But then all of a sudden we heard a rustling sound and Super Dog came running out of the bushes and everyone

Susie Keys threw the cheese sandwich up in the air and Super Dog jumped up really high and caught it in his mouth and everyone

We all stood in a circle around Super Dog and watched while he ate the cheese sandwich.

Once he was finished eating he sat down and **STARED** at Megan McNally.

That's when Megan said her **EYES** felt weird and that she thought Super Dog was trying to **COMMUNICATE** with her through his **EYES**.

So Megan put out her hand and Super Dog licked her hand four times and then ran away.

Then that afternoon when we were in PE Megan gasped because her **HAND ECZEMA RASH** had completely

DISAPPEARED.

Megan pointed to **EXACTLY** where Super Dog had licked her and said, **"LOOK!** It's not even **ITCHY** any more. Super Dog has

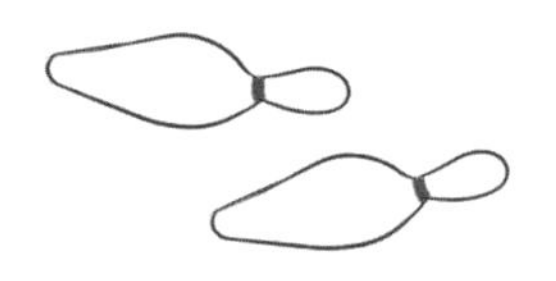

At afternoon break, we all **RAN** around the playground trying to find Super Dog until Susie Keys eventually found him sleeping in the long grass.

Jayden King said he had a bit of a tummy ache, so we told him to pet Super Dog and see what happened, so he did.

As **SOON** as Jayden touched Super Dog, he started smiling and said that he felt **MUCH** better and we all looked at each other because we knew how lucky we were to have Super Dog.

David Barry took his shoe and sock off and tried to get Super Dog to lick his foot that he'd hurt when he was playing football. But Super Dog got up and ran away.

EVERYONE blamed David Barry's smelly sock for making Super Dog run away and Susie Keys started crying because she was worried that David Barry's sock smelled **SO BAD** that Super Dog might have lost his **HEALING POWERS**.

When we got back to the classroom, Susie Keys was **STILL** crying and so we all had to tell Miss Riley about what was going on with Super Dog and all about the **FLYING** and **HEALING POWERS** and David Barry's

Miss Riley said that she was a hundred per cent sure the dog couldn't fly and that we must have just seen something else on the roof, like a seagull or something. Then she said that petting the dog probably just made Jayden **FORGET** about having a sore tummy and that Megan's **HAND ECZEMA** got better because she used her **SPECIAL HAND CREAM** from the doctors right after lunch.

Mr Harris went out into the playground to look for

Super Dog and when he came back he said, "The dog has moved on. There's nothing to worry about."

But we **WERE** worried because we had all -

with Super Dog and now he had moved on to heal people at other schools and we all missed him.

But then at the end of the day, when we were all waiting in the playground to get picked up, David Barry shouted, **"LOOK!"**

And we couldn't

BELIEVE IT!

Super Dog was **BACK** and he was standing **RIGHT** on top of Mr Harris's **CAR** and he was wearing a **CAPE** and it was blowing in the wind and **EVERYTHING!**

Mr Harris **STARED** at Super Dog and his mouth was **WIDE OPEN** because he obviously hadn't **BELIEVED** us before about Super Dog having

and being able to **FLY** and **HEAL** people.

But then all of a sudden, a lady came rushing into the school and shouted,

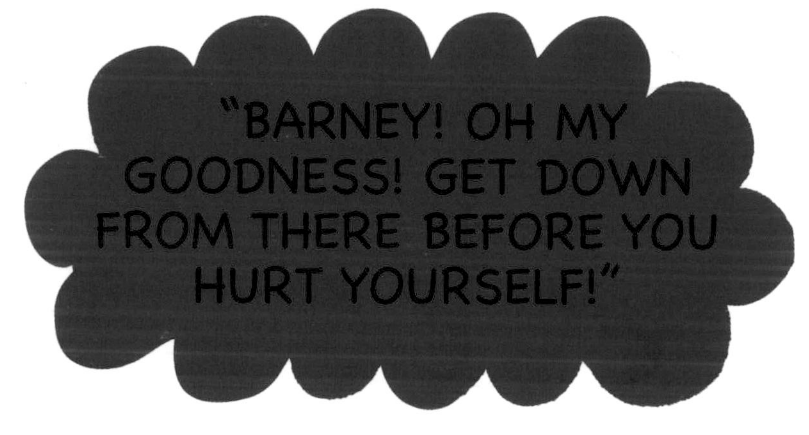

Super Dog did a

HUGE

leap and landed **RIGHT** next to Mr Harris who

SCREAMED

(because Mr Harris is a bit scared of dogs).

That's when Susie Keys said, "Who's Barney?"

The lady pointed to Super Dog and said that he was **HER** dog and that he was called Barney and that she'd been looking for him all day.

So we explained that he sort of belonged to us and our school now. And then we asked her if she knew he had powers.

THAT'S when the lady told us that Barney was a

VERY SPECIAL DOG

and that she didn't think he could fly but that he could **DEFINITELY** heal people.

She said that Barney was a **THERAPY DOG**, which meant that he is a dog that visits people in hospital and makes them feel better when they are ill.

So I said, "Are you **SURE** Barney can't fly?" because I didn't know how he had managed to get on top of Mr Harris's car if he couldn't fly and also because he had a **CAPE**.

But the lady said that it **WASN'T** a cape and that it was just a plastic bag that had got stuck in his collar, then she put Barney's lead on and started to leave.

Susie Keys said that **BARNEY** didn't really sound like a superhero name. But that's when Irfan Baxter said that Barney was probably just his **PRETEND** name because sometimes people with **POWERS** have **SECRET IDENTITIES**.

And that's when Barney turned round and gave us the **BIGGEST STARE** and barked for the **FIRST TIME** and we all **GASPED** and Mr Harris squealed a bit.

And we **KNEW** that meant Super Dog **COULD** fly and that he just didn't want loads of people to find out because it was a

SECRET.

THE MYSTERY MASH

One time we overheard one of the Year 6s say that the **POTATO MASH** at school dinners wasn't even made of **POTATO!**

Susie Keys zipped her coat RIGHT UP when she heard that, so that her coat was covering her mouth, and **REFUSED** to eat the rest of her sausages and mash.

Sunita Ram said that she didn't **BELIEVE** the Year 6s and that **OBVIOUSLY** the mash was made from potato because that's what mash is actually made from.

But then Irfan Baxter said,

No one **TOUCH** the mash!"

So we all froze, even Jayden King who had his fork halfway into his mouth.

That's when Irfan said the Year 6s were **ALWAYS** right and that if they knew that there was **NO POTATO** in the mash that it must be a **TRUE FACT**.

Irfan said, "We have no choice. We must do a **MYSTERY MASH INVESTIGATION.**"

Irfan said that someone needed to take a **SAMPLE** of the **MYSTERY MASH** and store it in their pencil case so we could do **EXPERIMENTS** on it.

Everyone **STARED** at the mash. But no one touched it because we were all too scared it might turn our skin green.

So Irfan took a deep breath, put Lauren Carr's gloves on, and used his fork to put some of the **MYSTERY MASH** inside his pencil case. And then we all ran out into the playground to do the **EXPERIMENTS**.

The first experiment Irfan said we should do was the **SNIFF TEST** because he said a **TASTE TEST** was

TOO DANGEROUS.

So we all stood in a line and sniffed the **MYSTERY MASH** and tried to guess what it was

REALLY

made of. But it didn't really smell of **ANYTHING** so that wasn't very helpful.

Irfan said that the second experiment was to look at the **MYSTERY MASH** under a **MICROSCOPE** to find out what it was made of. But we didn't have a microscope so we had to borrow Finola Smith's glasses, who is in the year below us, because she has

glasses. She says she can sometimes see aliens on the **MOON** at night.

THAT'S

how strong they are.

So Sunita Ram put on the glasses and went **RIGHT** up to the **MYSTERY MASH**. But then she said that she felt

and ran to the bathroom and Lauren Carr and Megan McNally ran after her.

Irfan said that the **MYSTERY MASH** must've looked

SO BAD

under the **MICROSCOPE GLASSES** that it made Sunita **PHYSICALLY SICK** and that

NOBODY

should look **DIRECTLY AT IT** and that we should all squint our eyes a bit when we looked at it, so we did.

Then Irfan took a deep breath and said that it was time for the **FINAL MYSTERY MASH EXPERIMENT** and that it was called the **SEAGULL TEST**.

Irfan said that seagulls eat **ALL FOOD** and that he knew that for a fact because his dad throws **ALL** their leftover food in to the garden and the seagulls eat it **ALL**, even the burnt bits.

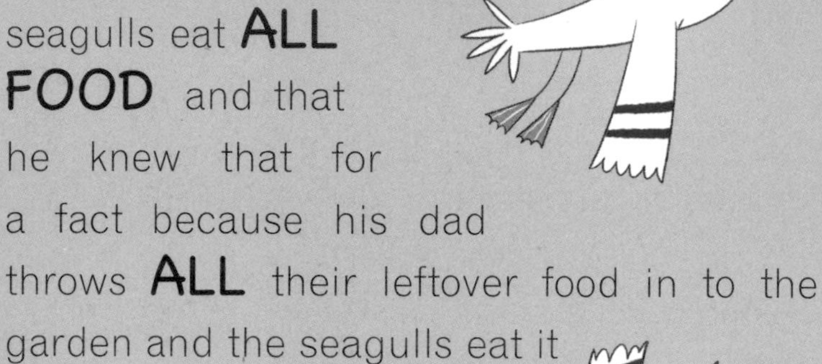

So we went over to where the seagulls usually sit and Irfan threw some of the Mystery Mash on the ground.

The seagulls went **WILD** when they saw it! But as **SOON** as they tasted it they began **SQUAWKING** really loudly and flew away.

That's when Irfan said, "Not even **SEAGULLS** will eat it. That must mean it's not real **FOOD!**"

We were all

when Irfan said that because we knew it was

TRUE

and because **WHO KNOWS** what we'd been eating at school dinners!

Miles McKay said he thought it was a **MIXTURE** of **WHITE PAINT** and **SAWDUST**.

But Susie Keys said it looked **JUST** like the stuff her dad used to fill the hole in her bedroom wall called **POLYFILLER** which is something builders use.

That's when **EVERYONE** started scraping their tongues because we couldn't **BELIEVE** that we had all been eating the **MYSTERY MASH** for years!

Irfan said we needed **EVIDENCE** if we were going to tell our mums and dads and maybe the Queen about what the dinner ladies were making us eat. And we all agreed.

So we sneaked towards the school canteen, and we made sure we stayed **CLOSE TO THE WALL** when we crossed the playground so the dinner ladies wouldn't see us coming and hide the **MYSTERY MASH**.

When we got to the kitchen **EVERYONE** was too scared to go inside until Finola Smith eventually said, "Fine. I'll go."

We were all

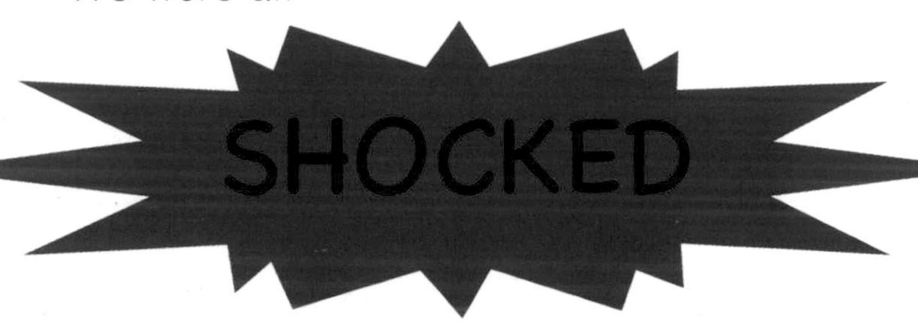

when Finola dropped to the floor and did a forward roll into the kitchen and hid behind the fridge, because we did not know that Finola had

because she was only in Year 2!

We all listened at the door but we couldn't hear anything for

AGES

so Irfan opened the door a bit and whispered, "Finola?"

But we didn't hear anything back. I was starting to get worried that Finola had maybe lost her glasses and wandered into one of the big fridges or something when all of a sudden she burst through the doors holding a

BIG TIN

that had "POTATO TASTE" written on it.

POTATO
TASTE

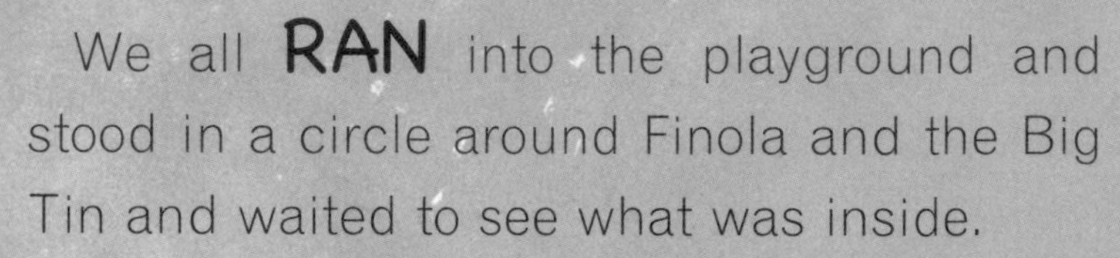

We all **RAN** into the playground and stood in a circle around Finola and the Big Tin and waited to see what was inside.

But **JUST** as Irfan was about to open it, one of the dinner ladies appeared and

GRABBED IT.

But Finola wouldn't let it go. Even when the dinner lady told her to!

The dinner lady tried to pull it out of Finola's hands and **THAT'S** when the lid came **FLYING** off and **LOADS** of **POWDER** came spilling out and went **EVERYWHERE!**

We all **SCREAMED** when the powder touched us because it looked **HORRIBLE** and **TOTALLY POISONOUS!**

Miss Riley and Mr Harris came running out to see what was going on and that's when Irfan shouted, **"HALT! COME NO FURTHER!** Or you'll get **CONTAMINATED!"**

But Mr Harris just ignored us and came **RIGHT** up to see what was going on and **THAT'S** when he saw the **"POTATO TASTE"** tin and we told him **ALL** about the **MYSTERY MASH**.

Miss Riley

when she heard what we said and then she looked **RIGHT** at Mr Harris and tutted and shook her head at him and that made him look a bit embarrassed.

Mr Harris told us that it was **POTATO POWDER** and **DEFINITELY** not

POISONOUS. But none of us believed him, so he stuck his finger in the tin and then put it in his mouth and said, "You see? I'm fine."

But he didn't **LOOK** fine. He looked exactly like Sunita Ram had looked when the **MYSTERY MASH** had made her sick!

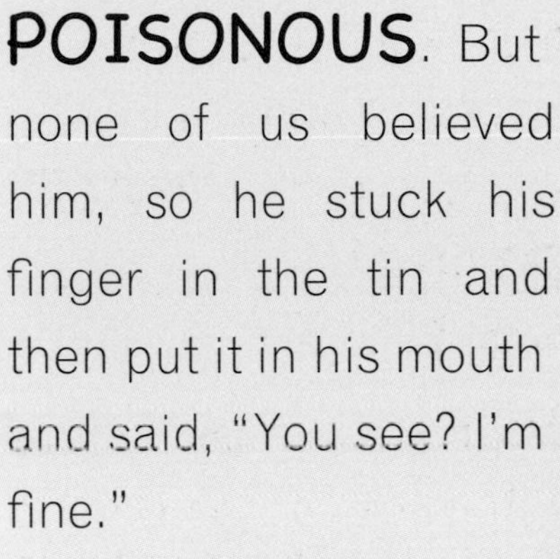

Once we were back in class, we asked Miss Riley about the **MYSTERY MASH** and she said, "It's definitely **NOT** poisonous."

And when Irfan asked if the **MYSTERY MASH** was made from potato, Miss Riley said, "Um ... sort of ... well... It's **POWDERED** potato."

Everyone **GASPED** because we **KNEW** that we'd been right! There was **NO ACTUAL POTATO** in the mash, just potato powder (which is **TOTALLY DISGUSTING!**). That's when Miss Riley told us that Mr Harris had bought the dinner ladies **POTATO POWDER** instead of **REAL** potatoes because it was **LESS EXPENSIVE** and also that it didn't taste very nice and that was probably why even seagulls wouldn't eat it. And then she said that Finola Smith's **GLASSES** had made Sunita feel sick because they were **TOO STRONG** for Sunita's eyes. And that we shouldn't wear other people's glasses.

That afternoon, we all got a letter home to give to our mums and dads and it said stuff like, **"I AM VERY SORRY"** and **"WE WILL ONLY SERVE REAL POTATOES AT SCHOOL DINNERS FROM NOW ON"** and **THAT'S** when we knew that we'd solved the **MYSTERY MASH CASE** and that all we had to do **NOW** was find out what was in those **WEIRD SAUSAGES!**

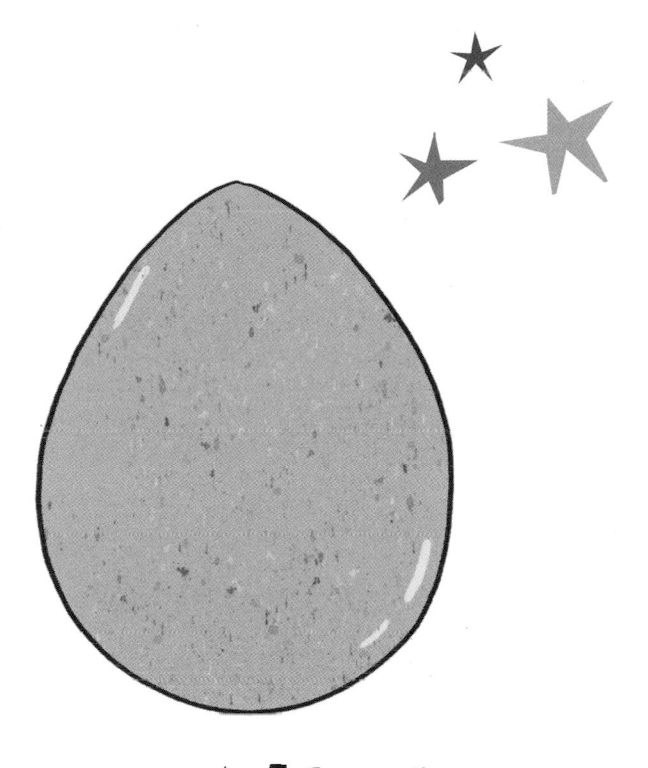

THE ALIEN EGG

FINALLY it was the School Sports Day and **EVERYONE** was excited about the Egg and Spoon race because that is everyone's **FAVOURITE** Sports Day activity.

But we were all very **SUSPICIOUS** of Susie Keys because she was being **REALLY WEIRD** about her **EGG** and she wouldn't let **ANYONE** come near it.

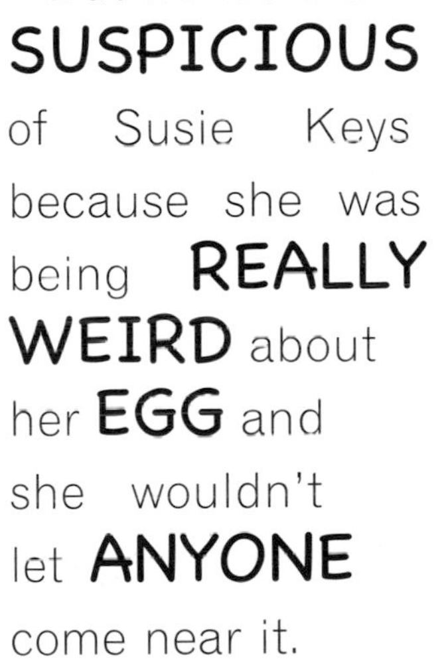

Miss Riley said, "I think we should all name our eggs this year. Just for fun!"

So we all made up names for the eggs Miss Riley had given us.

I called mine Helen and Miles Mckay called his Bob.

Other people picked names like Splat and Eggy McEggerson and Samantha. But when it was Susie's turn to pick an egg and name it she said that she'd brought her **OWN**

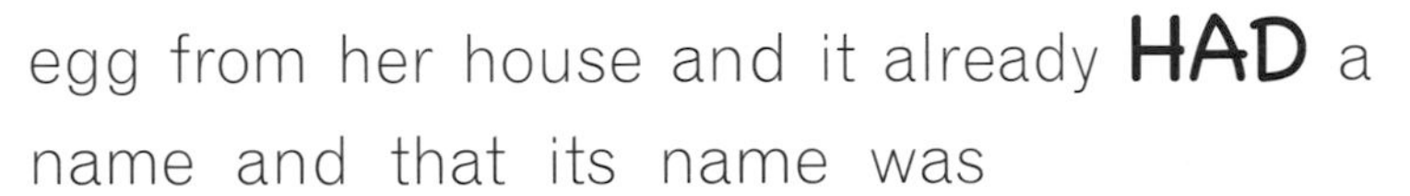

egg from her house and it already **HAD** a name and that its name was **TARZOCK**.

We all thought that was a pretty **WEIRD** name for an egg but nobody said anything because the bell for morning break rang.

Everyone left their eggs in the classroom at break. But Susie Keys didn't. She held it in her hands and walked up and down the playground with it, which we all thought was **STRANGE**.

Joel Jack tried to **TOUCH** Susie's egg when we were lining up in the playground after break and Susie screamed,

And we all gasped.

After break, we all decided that the reason Susie was being so **WEIRD** about her egg, and why she didn't want anyone to touch it, was because she was a **CHEATER**.

Joel Jack said that he thought Susie Keys had **BOILED** her egg and turned it into a super-strong **HARD-BOILED** egg so that if it fell during the Egg and Spoon race she'd be able to pick it up and keep on going because hard-boiled eggs don't break.

We all agreed and as soon as Susie Keys wasn't looking we stuck a tiny pin from Lauren Carr's badge into the egg to see if **LIQUID EGG** would come out so we could have **PROOF** that the egg was **HARD-BOILED**.

And liquid **DID** come out, so that meant that the egg **WASN'T** hard-boiled and that Susie Keys **WASN'T** a **CHEATER**.

But then Joel Jack's face went a bit funny and he pointed at the egg and said, "Um... Why is it **GREEN**?"

We all looked at the tiny bit of gooey liquid that was coming out of the egg. It **WAS** green!

But then Susie came back from Miss Riley's desk so we had to all run back to our seats and pretend that we hadn't been doing anything.

At lunch, Joel Jack went completely **WHITE** and said, "I think I know why the egg is green and why Susie won't let anyone come near it... It's an **ALIEN EGG**!"

That's when Jayden King **SQUEALED** because his most scary thing **EVER** is **ALIENS** and he gave Susie Keys **SUCH** a fright that she **DROPPED THE ALIEN EGG!**

The egg **ROLLED** right across the dining centre and Susie **SCREAMED**,

"TARZOCK! NOOOOOOOOO!"

and dropped her tray and ran after it.

When the egg **EVENTUALLY** stopped rolling Susie picked it up and **HUGGED IT FOR AGES** and began speaking to it in some sort of **WEIRD ALIEN LANGUAGE** and we were all

SHOCKED.

After lunch, everyone was a bit nervous about Sports Day because of the **ALIEN EGG**.

When it was time for the **EGG AND SPOON** race **NO ONE** wanted to take part because we were all **TERRIFIED** that Susie Keys' **ALIEN EGG** would hatch and **SLIME US ALL TO DEATH!**

But Miss Riley made us all get our eggs and spoons out and told us not to be **SHY** just because our parents were watching and that she **BELIEVED IN US**.

So we all put our **NORMAL, NON-ALIEN** eggs on our spoons and waited for the whistle to blow.

As soon as Mr Harris blew the Official Whistle, Susie Keys went **RACING** down the pitch with her egg and spoon while everyone else just walked **REALLY**

SLOWLY about **ONE MILLION MILES** behind her because we were all terrified of her **EGG**.

When Susie Keys crossed the finish line the crowd **CHEERED** and she got **SO** excited that she'd won **FIRST PLACE** that she threw **BOTH** hands in the air and the egg hit the ground with a

We all **SCREAMED** and ducked for cover when the alien egg cracked because we knew that the

was about to **HATCH!**

But no one else seemed to notice about the egg, except us and Susie Keys, until the

The alien egg had **SPLATTERED** all over the ground and there was green alien goo **EVERYWHERE** and it was

STINKING!

Susie Keys screamed, “He’s **DEAD!** Tarzock my lucky egg is

DEAD!”

Miss Riley held her nose and said, "Susie! How **OLD** was that egg? It's completely **ROTTEN!**"

That's when Susie said that the egg was exactly **ONE YEAR OLD** and that it was the same egg she had used **LAST YEAR** when she came Third Place and that she had kept it all year, and called it Tarzock, because it was her

egg and she knew she could win First Place if she used it again this year.

Miss Riley looked like she was going to be **SICK** when she heard Susie say that the egg was a **WHOLE YEAR OLD**, and she even covered her mouth with her hand a bit.

That's when Joel Jack said, "We thought it was an **ALIEN EGG** that had special powers to help you win the race!"

Susie cheered up a bit when Joel Jack told her that because she thought it was **HILARIOUS** that we thought her lucky egg was an **ALIEN** egg.

We explained about the egg having an **ALIEN NAME** and the

WEIRD

ALIEN LANGUAGE we heard her speaking to the egg, and **THAT** made her laugh even **HARDER!**

Susie said that she named her lucky egg after her two favourite things joined together: Tarzan and her cat called Socks. That's how she came up with the name **TARZOCK**.

Then Susie said that she wasn't speaking to the egg in a **WEIRD ALIEN LANGUAGE** and that she probably sounded weird because she was using her **BABY TALK** voice that she uses to speak to cute things like babies and kittens.

STAR CHART
FOOD HYGIENE
SPELLING

For the rest of the afternoon, Miss Riley gave us all a **BIG TALK** about **FOOD HYGIENE** and how food is **NOT** a good luck charm **OR** a pet, and then she went on for ages about how we **DEFINITELY SHOULDN'T** keep an egg for a year. Then she had to sit down for a bit because she looked like she was going to faint.

That's when we said sorry to Susie about the **SPLAT-DEATH** of her **LUCKY EGG**. But Susie said that it was OK because she actually had **ANOTHER EGG** from when she was in Year 1 and that she could use that next year.

And we all

Also by PAMELA BUTCHART and
illustrated by BECKA MOOR

PTO for a
SNEAK PEEK!

WIGGLESBOTTOM PRIMARY
THE MAGIC HAMSTER

Everyone went **WILD** when Miss Riley introduced us to the new class pet because we'd NEVER had a class pet before and also because it was a

HAMSTER.

wanted to choose the hamster's name and Anne-Marie Moor wouldn't stop shouting

Miss Riley told us that everyone was allowed to put **ONE** name in the "Hamster Name Suggestion Box".

Everyone crossed their fingers and legs for luck when Miss Riley reached into the box and pulled out a name.

But when she read the name she looked a bit cross. And then she said, "Anne-Marie, how many suggestions did you put into the suggestion box?" But Anne-Marie wouldn't answer, and we knew it was because she'd probably put loads in.